Sweet Getaways

SHORT ROMANCE STORIES ABOUT LOVE ON HOLIDAY

ERICA ANOE

For everyone seeking renewal and refreshment

I haven't been everywhere, but it's on my list.

SUSAN SONTAG

Contents

Introduction

I had so much fun writing *Sweet Beginnings: Short Romance Stories About New Love* that I realized I wanted to make it a series. It's a wonderful thing to spend time with characters awash in the hope and possibility that comes with new love.

For this installment, however, I decided to focus on getaways. Like beginnings, getaways often bring life into sharp focus. Colors become vivid when away from home. The habits of ordinary life loosen, and it's easier to contemplate what else we might be doing with ourselves and our precious lives.

In situations like this, magic can happen. Moments can strike that take us beyond brief periods of relaxation. In this open, creative, easy state, we may become more open to love.

Sweet Getaways includes several stories of couples at the beginning of their story together. "Unexpected Guest" touches on the glimmer of possibility that appears when you're not even quite sure it's really a date. "Layover" brings a woman a chance to explore an evening with an old crush.

However, I also took the liberty of going beyond beginnings. "Beachside Resort" tells the story of a lifetime of longing come to fruition. "The Worst Trip Ever" describes the beginning of a lifetime commitment.

Finally, in "Happily Ever After," a woman reflects on a lifetime of love and what it means to her to face mortality.

If you like the stories in Sweet Getaways, read on for a bonus story from Sweet Beginnings.

I hope these stories bring you comfort and hope and renew your own sense of possibility.

- *Erica Anoe, July 2022*

Unexpected Guest

Beth Jefferson finally found the driveway for her vacation rental, barely visible in the darkness, and pulled in. She hadn't meant to arrive so late – her plane had been hours delayed, and then, even after she picked up her bag and left the airport, the rental car's GPS had taken her on a winding route through three separate construction zones.

In the darkness, shapes that had been appealing in the photographs she'd seen online took on an air of unexpected menace – large leaves with heavy fronds that bent under their own weight, thick stands of fruit trees surrounded by the smell of rot and a mountain looming over it all. The hulking mass of an old SUV shadowed the end of the driveway.

Much as Beth wanted to get inside and start her vacation, she felt reluctant to open the car door and get out. Something about the place didn't feel right, and she couldn't put her finger on why.

"It probably doesn't feel right because you're tired and dehydrated," she said out loud, trying to soothe herself. Still, she took out her phone and triple-checked the address, her confirmation email and the instructions for getting inside.

All she needed to do was enter the code into the box next to the front door. It wouldn't take long, and then she'd be inside, and the place would be nice, and she could start relaxing.

"You can do this," she whispered to herself. Beth took a deep breath, snapped the driver's side door open and ran around to the trunk for her bag.

As much as the driveway gave her the creeps, there was a fresh note in the air that reminded her of why she'd come to this place. The night was louder than she'd expected, full of crickets and frogs, but she found the sound comforting – it wasn't the silence that she'd feared would creep her out. She could smell the not-so-distant ocean. She'd managed to leave the city and its grime behind.

Beth eased her bag out of the trunk and set it heavily on the driveway, feeling the spongy earth beneath the gravel give. It was good to be here already – and it would get better.

She rolled the bag toward the front door. Beth's rental was a small cottage, no more than 500 square feet inside. It was surrounded on all sides by thick stands of trees, and light pooling from its windows made it seem like a small, friendly sanctuary in the middle of unspoiled nature.

Beth told herself that her lingering unease came simply because she wasn't used to places like this. She'd lived most of her life in downtown apartments, and the idea that there was nothing around her but plants and wildlife wasn't exactly comfortable – even if she'd wanted to have this experience.

She had the money, and she had vacation days to spare. What she didn't have was motivation to get away from work and her normal life. Beth always found reasons not to take trips and not to relax or have fun. But this trip was different. This was the result of her resolution to get herself the rest she needed and deserved.

She took a deep breath, pulled up the entry code on her phone and began typing it in.

The door swung open before she could finish entering the sequence of numbers.

Standing in the doorway of Beth's vacation rental, backlit by the warm light of the cottage, was a man out of a magazine ad, the kind that promised relaxation by the beach if you drank the right margarita. He was shirtless, allowing Beth to see each individual abdominal muscle – not to mention pecs and a bunch of arm muscles she couldn't even name. He blinked sleepily, revealing golden brown eyes and thick, dark lashes. His hair was dark, wavy and shaggy in the way that always made Beth wonder if he was late getting a haircut or choosing that length on purpose.

Beth had a sudden inappropriate urge to ask him to turn around so she could see his back, but this was a man, not a statue. And he was a man inside the cottage that was supposed to be her vacation rental – she should be alarmed, not fascinated.

"Who are you?" she asked. Her voice sounded embarrassingly breathless, and she was glad to think the darkness would hide the way her face and neck heated when she met his gaze.

He groaned and ran a hand through his hair. It took serious mental focus for Beth to keep her eyes from focusing on his ripping arm muscles. "Damn it, you're a paying customer, yeah?"

"What are you talking about?"

"Sorry. I'm Keola Kahale. My uncle owns this cottage, and he doesn't mind if I stay in it when it's not rented to someone." He winced. "I should have checked the calendar before I came to crash."

Beth blinked, processing the situation. "I'm just going to text your uncle to make sure you're not, like, a serial killer pretending to be a nephew."

Keola's face took on a pained expression, but he said, "Yeah, I get it."

"What's the matter?" Beth asked, pausing in the midst of typing the text.

"He'll be pissed. But I know you need to look out for yourself."

She lowered the phone. "I don't want to get you in trouble."

"I don't want to make you uncomfortable."

Beth had the urge to offer to let him stay, but it was a tiny place, and she didn't know him from Adam. No matter how hot he was, that was a stupid idea.

"Listen," he said. "I can find somewhere else to crash tonight. If you just give me a few minutes to clear out, I'll be out of your hair." He peered out at the driveway. "I might need you to move your car, but you'll have your vacation rental all to yourself."

She stared at the SUV she'd parked behind, which she'd assumed was out of commission. "That's your vehicle?" Keola gave a short laugh. "She runs. Gotta duct tape her back together once a week or so, but she gets me where I need to go."

Beth hesitated. His offer made sense, and she did need to be able to sleep in the place she'd booked, but something wasn't sitting right again. "Where are you going to go? You're crashing here for a reason, right?"

His face reddened, and he looked away from her.

For one wild, irrational moment, she felt a surge of jealousy as she imagined him going to sleep with some woman he knew. Whoever she was, she was probably local, beautiful – the sort of woman with hair to her waist and curves to spare, not crisp and sporty like Beth. Keola's women probably wore island-style dresses and graceful sandals, not khaki shorts and tennis shoes and polo shirts they'd been given at work. Beth did her best to get hold of her mind before it raced miles down the track of comparing herself with Keola's hypothetical girlfriend.

But he didn't say anything about a woman. Instead, he shrugged and said, "It's a nice night. The beach will be fine." He held up a hand. "No, don't look at me like that. I've done it before. It's not a big deal. And I'm not homeless, if that's what you're wondering. I live on Oahu, downtown in Honolulu, but sometimes I fly to Maui to take a break. That old SUV's been here for me since I was a teenager growing up here. It's a different pace of life on this island. Perfect for when I need to get away and forget about spreadsheets and KPIs and whatever."

Beth gave a surprised laugh. The corner of Keola's mouth lifted. "You thought I was a homeless beach bum sort of nephew."

She opened her mouth to deny it, but then shut it without saying anything. She knew any lie she tried to come up with would sound weak. "I maybe thought that. I also thought it was funny how much you sound like me. I also flew to Maui to forget about spreadsheets and KPIs."

"I'm surprised you didn't go to Waikiki."

"I was looking for less of a city experience."

"Yeah? What are you planning to do here?"

Beth crossed her arms over her chest, feeling sheepish.

"I'm not a country girl in any way, don't get me wrong. But I like to fish."

Keola raised an eyebrow. "If you're not a country girl, where are you fishing?"

"A river runs right through the middle of the city where I live. It's maybe a 15 minute walk from my apartment. I wouldn't *eat* any of the fish I catch in that river, so I just throw them back. But there's something about sitting there on a Saturday morning. You're in the sun, but you're doing something. You have something to pay attention to. I thought it might be nice to try it here."

Keola grinned. "I would not have guessed fishing would be your answer?"

"What *would* you have guessed?"

He leaned back against the doorframe, crossing his arms, studying her with exaggerated seriousness. "Horseback riding," he said finally. "I see that designer luggage. You look like the kind of girl who came here to take long guided tours through the rainforest on horseback."

"That actually sounds like a good idea," Beth said. "I should have thought of that."

They both laughed.

"Well," Keola said. He held the doorframe with one hand and swung lazily from side to side. The gesture made him seem boyish and shy, and Beth found herself smiling affectionately at him, having to remind herself again that she didn't really know him. "I can't take you horseback riding... but I can take you fishing. If you're interested."

"I was going to rent poles and stuff."

"I can cover that if you're okay with it. Pay you back for messing up your arrival at your vacation rental."

"It's not that messed up."

"No?" Keola said, eyes dancing. His expression made

her feel like she'd revealed more than she meant to. Heat ran down Beth's neck and onto her chest.

"Not messed up at all," Beth said decisively.

"Give me a few minutes to clear out," Keola said, "and then I'll see you in the morning. 5:30 if you think you can handle it."

His voice was low and full of promise. His tone made her feel like they were talking about something much dirtier than fishing. "I can handle it," Beth said, and to her delight, she sounded confident and sure of herself.

She watched with some disappointment as Keola stepped back into the living room and pulled his T-shirt off an old orange couch. Beth mentally wished his abs good night and comforted herself with the thought that she had a good chance of seeing them again in the morning – he'd probably want to take his shirt off again as the day heated up.

Beth settled into a yellow-cushioned chair beside the couch that seemed about as old as she was, but she didn't mind the age of the furniture. It was cozy inside the cottage, just the sort of sanctuary the pool of light had promised. She could already tell that waking up here would be spectacular. She jingled her keys in one hand, waiting for him to be ready for her to let him out of the driveway.

Keola shoved a book and a cell phone charger into a backpack and gave Beth a nod. She stood, and they walked out of the cottage together.

It felt oddly natural to walk beside him. It wasn't hard to imagine reaching out a few inches to twine her fingers with his. She thought about how much they had in common – similar jobs, it sounded like, and a love of fishing.

Keola stroked the top of the SUV before letting himself

into it, a gesture she found endearing. Beth was looking forward to spending time with him, and the anticipation of "what if" had started a pleasant fizzy feeling in her chest, as if she'd had a glass of champagne.

"I'll see you tomorrow," he said as he got into the vehicle, and she drank in the way the words made her feel.

Beachside Resort

"It's a great deal, I said. How hot can it be, I said. Look at those low prices, I said. It's a beachside resort, I said. Did you *tell* me I was an idiot?"

Clayton Ramos, the poor bastard I'd convinced to come with me on this trip, was kind enough not to say anything. Instead, he let out a sympathetic groan.

Above us, the air conditioner whined with little output, like a teenager more interested in complaining than in doing chores.

I moaned and threw my arms over my head, but the gesture made me feel even hotter and stickier, so instead I moved them to my sides and tried to think cooling thoughts.

I was lying on one of two "full" beds in our "beachside resort" – "full" in scare quotes because both mattresses seemed oddly short, and "beachside" because if you stood on your tiptoes and found just the right angle for your neck and managed to do this without throwing out your lower back and doubling over, you could see the tiniest sliver of

Gulf Coast beach from our window. I had no idea how they justified "resort."

The bed was older than I was, and it reacted to any movement I made with an arthritic groan. Its idea of support was simply being under me. I was pretty sure my back would hurt less if I slept in the bathtub.

When I glanced over at Clayton, he had his eyes closed and his phone pressed to his forehead. I could see rivulets of sweat dripping from his forehead, down his temples, and into his thick, tightly curled black hair.

"Why are you doing that with your phone?" I asked.

"The screen feels cool."

"Ugh, this is ridiculous. There has to be something we can do."

"It's Florida in August. The only thing we could do is check out of here and find somewhere more expensive with a better air conditioner."

"What about the KFC down the street? They have air conditioning, surely."

Clayton sat up, swiping ineffectually at the sweat on his forehead. Some of it dripped into his eyes and he winced and blinked rapidly. He looked utterly miserable, and it made me feel terrible to see it. The expression he turned on me was bleak and hopeless, made all the more stark by the stunning cat-like striations of his irises. "I tried to go there this morning before you woke up. The dining room is closed indefinitely due to staffing shortages."

Which was pretty much the story of this town. It had been a hard couple years all over the world, and I understood that. This was the sort of vacation destination that had been much more popular several decades ago, before interstates had bypassed it and people had become more comfortable traveling farther from home. It had probably been only barely hanging on before the recent downturn and worldwide difficulties.

But I'd hatched the stupid idea of coming here because it seemed affordable (with the help of a traveling companion to split costs with me).

I'd failed to convince my female friends that some time at a beachside resort was just what we needed. I'd shown them the website, read the blurb out loud: "Luxuriate in the lazy heat of an ocean-side room."

("In *Florida*? In *August*?" my friend Lily had said – and I now felt a little angry at her. Couldn't she have tried harder to make me understand what she meant?)

In desperation, I'd turned to my brother. But Tom had just started dating someone new, and sharing a room with his sister in a small town on the Florida Gulf Coast was understandably less appealing to him than spending every waking moment – and a lot of moments he probably shouldn't have been awake – in bed with Toby.

As luck would have it, Clayton had been over at Tom's place when I'd made the proposal. "I'll go with you," Clayton had said suddenly, casually, as if he was offering to accompany me to the corner store.

I'd stopped pressuring Tom immediately and looked at Clayton. He and Tom had been friends since we were kids, and I still remembered when Clayton started growing an adolescent beard and I spent an entire dinner trying not to stare too obviously at the scattering of hairs along his jawline. When he finally caught me looking, he'd blushed as if I'd mocked him, but the truth was that I found it unbelievably attractive. I pushed my noodles around on my plate that entire dinner, not really able to chew and swallow, grappling with feelings I couldn't define or name – feelings that had something to do with Clayton Ramos's jaw and mouth.

Those feelings about Clayton, that desire to stare at him, had never really gone away. But we were adults now. He'd graduated from adolescent beard to 5 o'clock shadow, and he had a man's hands and a slower smile than when we were kids. He'd grown into the long, gangly limbs he'd had as a teenager. Clayton now was tall and strong. He'd hurt his back working for a moving company, but he still managed to coach football at the local Boys and Girls Club.

I'd learned how to dress up and wear makeup but then had gotten tired of it and stopped, and I'd moved in with a serious boyfriend and back out again. I'd been promoted to a fancy title at the nonprofit where I worked – though the pay still didn't match what I could have made at the local Chick-Fil-A. I'd been told I had a nice body by men I did and didn't believe, but I'd decided for myself that it was nice. I looked at myself every morning in the mirror and told myself so, hands stroking the curve of a belly that the world told me I should rid myself of at any cost.

Now Clayton was offering to travel to Florida with me, and I had to wonder if he'd been looking at me all this time, too.

"You sure?" I asked.

He shrugged and grinned. The way my insides flipped over when he did that struck me as a sign that this was either the best or the worst idea ever.

And I wanted – needed – to get out of town for a while, and I was sure Clayton could pay for his half of the trip. "Okay," I said. "Let's do it."

He answered with a happy laugh that made me want to do it right now.

Unfortunately, in this decaying town of vacations past,

in a shitty motel room that invited scare quotes when describing anything it might contain, that happy laugh couldn't have seemed farther away.

The selfish part of me had hoped for something more festive. Or relaxing. Or positive in any way.

Positive was not feeling deep disappointment that the KFC dining room was closed or searching online for the nearest public library and wanting to scream endlessly at the discovery that it was closed, too.

I'd have suggested we go to the beach and get in the water, but we'd done that all day yesterday, until even our brown skin had begun to burn. Besides, the ocean was disturbingly warm, the temperature and texture of milk left on the counter too long.

"I'm sorry this trip sucks so much," I told Clayton.

His jaw worked. I could see that he wanted to tell me it didn't suck, but that he couldn't manage to summon the lie.

"You don't have to pretend," I said. "It really, really sucks."

"It was fun in the car on the way down," Clayton said.

"Really?" We'd taken turns driving and playing music and kept the windows rolled down to save gas. We'd traded tips for the cheapest and most satisfying orders at the fast food restaurants where we stopped for food. I'd practiced not staring at him, no matter how fascinating I found his face. But I hadn't picked up any particular emotion from him – just a sense of ease.

"You let me play Sepultura." His voice was serious, as if there was a hidden, consequential meaning to this.

I shrugged. "It was your turn."

"I've never met a girl – woman – who let me play that."

I couldn't help but shiver at the emphasis he placed on

the word *woman*, but I kept my tone light for my response. "You let me play Bollywood hits."

"It was cool to hear stuff I never heard before."

"That's how I felt about Sepultura."

He raised an eyebrow, and I spread my arms innocently. I had nothing to hide.

"I didn't hate it," I said honestly.

"It was a fun drive," he said with a definitive nod.

"I just wish I could figure out how to have fun now," I groaned, closing my eyes. "I'm so hot I can't even think straight, and I feel so bad that I brought you here. And now I know why it was so cheap to get a room here, and I feel really dumb, and–"

I stopped talking abruptly because Clayton came and sat on the bed next to me. The mattress dipped so much under his weight that we were practically on the floor now, but the shock of that was nothing compared to the shock of him taking my hand in one of his.

His fingers and palm were rough and calloused. I had to clench my jaw to stop my teeth from chattering. He waited a few beats, giving me a chance to speak or pull my hand away. Then he pulled it toward him, bringing both our hands to rest on top of his thigh.

My heart began to clatter against my rib cage. The air – already hot and thick – seemed too liquid for me to pull it easily into my lungs when I breathed in. I lifted my head to look at him, feeling I needed visual confirmation that Clayton Ramos was actually holding my hand, that my fingers were inches away from his jeans and the muscled thigh beneath them.

"Monica," he said. "Stop feeling bad about me. Unless you're sorry I'm here, I'm not sorry."

"You're not? Are you sure this isn't heatstroke talking?"

"I've never had the chance to spend time with you like this before," Clayton said softly.

I thought I understood what he was trying to tell me, but my brain couldn't quite accept it. Instead, I continued to lament my planning failures. "I wish it weren't so miserable here."

He shook my hand gently where it rested in his lap. "Why are you miserable? What can I do?"

"Give me an ice bath?"

He didn't answer my suggestion with words. Instead, his eyes darkened and that slow smile he'd grown into spread across his face. Something stirred inside me, as mysterious and unnameable as what I felt about him when I was young. I always thought that feeling was so deep and strange because of the intensity of teenage hormones, but I couldn't remember feeling this way with the boyfriend I'd lived with. I started to wonder if this feeling might have more to do with Clayton Ramos than I'd previously allowed.

I pressed my lips together, my throat suddenly dry. Clayton was looking at my mouth. The room felt even hotter than before, but I didn't mind this temperature increase.

"Why did you come on this trip?"

He adjusted his hold of my hand, tightening the way his fingers laced through mine. "It did sound good to get out of town and go to the beach," Clayton said carefully. But before I could respond to the neutral statement, he lifted his free hand. I waited, breath coming faster. "But if the person suggesting the trip wasn't Monica Pearson... I don't know if I would have agreed so quickly."

"Do you regret it?"

"Do you?"

I squeezed my eyes shut. "Only when I think the trip sucks so much that you wish you weren't here."

"I don't wish that."

His tone of voice was low and intimate. I shifted a few inches closer to him, wanting to close the gap between us but still searching for the courage.

When I spoke, my voice had taken on a throaty rasp that made me sound older and sexier than I felt. "Do you remember the time you found me drunk at that party and drove me home?"

"Of course."

"I spent the whole drive wishing you would kiss me."

"I wouldn't have done that when you were drunk."

"I know," I said. "But I did sort of think you wanted to."

"Do you remember the dress you had on? Anyone would have wanted to."

I smiled at him. The air conditioner kicked loudly above us and the noise startled me. I'd forgotten about the discomfort of the room. Instead, I was enjoying the sudden freedom I felt to stare into Clayton's eyes, admire his cheekbones, speculate about his lips.

"Have you ever wished something like that since then? That I would kiss you?"

"I've wished it plenty of times."

The slow smile widened.

"When was the last time?"

"One second ago."

Clayton's free hand came to rest against the side of my face, brushed my hair away from my eyes.

"Please," I whispered.

He kissed the corner of my mouth lightly, his breath hot against my skin. Then he kissed the other side. Impatient, I turned my mouth fully against his.

And this kiss that we'd wanted for years transformed the room, the town, the trip. As I wound my arms around his neck and slipped my fingers into his hair, I didn't care about the heat or the quality of the room or whether KFC was open. I tasted ocean salt on his lips, smelled sun on his skin.

The kiss went on forever, as Clayton and I luxuriated in the lazy heat of our beachside resort.

Layover

It was not Natalie's most attractive moment.

She'd been running for her connecting flight, running with everything she had, running until it felt like her calves would seize and mutiny and a knife had slid into her ribs and her breath, like the plane, was something that could not be caught. She'd felt her backpack slamming into her lower back with each step, the corner of a hardback bruising her through the thick material. She'd nearly run over old ladies and little kids and she was pretty sure she'd bumped into more than a few people.

And all that to come up to the gate gasping, just moments after the doors had closed, to see the gate attendants stop joking with each other and shake their heads sadly at the sight of her. To still not be able to catch her breath, no matter how hard she tried, partly because she'd been neglecting the gym and partly because it was so difficult to catch her breath while also fighting off threatening sobs.

A young, small part of her wanted to throw herself to the floor then and there and wail and cry her guts out until someone fixed it all for her, got her on the plane she needed to be on, made the disastrous business trip she'd just taken go well after all and made sure she got home safe.

But Natalie was a 32-year-old woman, and she knew her mother was not about to magically show up at the airport to make it all better. So she tried to breathe, and she tried to compose her face to look less upset than she felt, and she looped her fingers through the straps of her backpack and clutched it tightly and nodded as if she understood the things the airline staff were saying to her.

"Ma'am," one of them said, snapping his fingers. "Are you all right? Do you need some water? Do you need to sit down?"

"Yeah," Natalie managed, and collapsed into the nearest row of chairs as if a string that had been holding her up was suddenly cut.

She had questions. She needed to figure out what plane they could put her on and when she could get home, but her heart was hammering against her sternum and her pulse was pounding against her ear.

And apparently she was also having hallucinations, because she could have sworn that the man approaching the gate with a hopeless expression was Garret Grant, as in captain of the crew team in college, as in upper arms that would have made Chris Hemsworth jealous, as in Natalie's college crush.

If she'd believed this was really him, she would have been ashamed for him to see her this way – sweating, panting, nearly crying, hair messed up, makeup probably running from the sweat. Natalie, however, sat numbly, thinking she was staring at a man who happened to look like Garret – a ridiculously attractive man with a similar build and with a tan and muscles that promised he still rowed.

She watched as he walked slowly toward the gate attendants. Everything about him spoke of success – that suit was no Men's Wearhouse special, and the shoes had probably cost as much as the suit. But he dangled his designer briefcase forlornly from one hand, and the gesture pierced Natalie's heart. It made her think of a three-year-old. It reminded her of how she felt.

"I gave up on running," the man was saying. "I'm too late, aren't I?"

"We're too late," Natalie interjected from where she sat. She wasn't in the habit of talking to strangers, but she felt the need to establish solidarity with him.

After all, they both needed to get to Atlanta. They were both stuck in Detroit.

In a situation like this, in the middle of an airport, those two facts were enough to establish a fast friendship.

He turned toward her and there was no denying it anymore. This was Garret, only older and somehow more handsome, his lips firmer and more determined than she recalled, but his green eyes just as full of mischief. Before she could say his name, he was saying hers.

"Natalie? Natalie Reynolds?"

It made her grin that he remembered. She'd never quite been sure he knew she existed.

She stood up, and that was the moment it sunk in that she probably looked terrible. She scraped a limp dark curl off her forehead. "Sorry – I've been up since 3 a.m." She wasn't sure what she was apologizing for exactly – not wearing an evening gown? Looking like she felt?

He looked expectant, and it occurred to Natalie that he might be wondering if she remembered him. "Chem major," she said. "You led the crew team to being top in the conference for the first time in more than two decades." The expression on his face hadn't eased, and she shook her head and said, "Everyone knew your name, Garret. Anyone would remember you."

"You two went to college together?" asked the gate attendant, reminding Natalie of her existence.

"Yeah," Natalie said. "Go Hawks!"

"Now we're hoping to go to Atlanta together," Garret cut in. "What have you got for us?"

The gate attendant winced. She somehow did this without wrinkling the skin of her face. She was so smooth and perfectly made up, it was almost as if she'd ironed her face along with her uniform. "I hate to tell you, but the plane that just left–"

"Was the last flight to Atlanta today," Natalie cut in. She'd feared as much already. It was part of why she'd run so hard.

Not that it was a disaster to get home a day late – she could call her friend Anna and ask her to feed her cat another day, and work would have to understand because they were the reason she was on this plane to begin with. It was just that, after the way this trip had gone, she'd been longing for the comfort of her own bed.

"I can get you both on a flight for 10:20 a.m. tomorrow. That's the earliest I can do. Everything else is booked."

"And what about accommodations?" Garret asked, leaning closer. The way he said "accommodations" stirred something in Natalie. He made it sound sophisticated and sensual. When he said it, she pictured sitting in a hot tub with a glass of sherry, not trying to find the right pillow in a dingy airport hotel with only three hours to actually sleep.

The gate attendant must have felt it, too. A blush crept

up the sides of her neck. Natalie felt an unexpected stab of jealousy, then grinned at her foolishness. Garret Grant was and had always been way out of her league.

Even now, he looked like a successful businessman. Natalie wasn't sure if "Just Lost a Major Client" was a look people could identify in her face and clothes, but it was the reality of her career at the moment. This trip had been a last-ditch effort to save the account, and her boss had been convinced it would be worth it, but in fact, Natalie had simply failed again. She'd had a string of awkward meetings in Austin, culminating in one really awkward one where the client had told her they'd decided to go with a different agency for their design needs.

"You know what I could use is a drink," Natalie said out loud. "And accommodations, too, after the drink," she said quickly.

"I can help with that," the gate attendant said with an insincere smile. "Drink tickets and a voucher for the airport hotel. I'm seeing that both of you landed after the cutoff time within which we consider it possible for you to have made your connection."

"It may not be the MGM Grand," Garret said smoothly, "but I'll take it."

"Um, I'll take it also," Natalie said.

The gate attendant began to fill out forms, muttering to herself. Natalie was left shifting from foot to foot, sneaking glances at Garret. Probably he was tired after a long day of travel. He likely wanted to be left alone, not be suddenly stuck with an acquaintance from his college days as a traveling companion.

When the gate attendant handed them each drink tickets and a voucher, as well as a hygiene kit since they wouldn't have access to their checked luggage, Garret and Natalie turned to each other.

"About that drink..." he said, at the same moment she said, "I should probably get a Lyft."

He raised a sharp, blond eyebrow. "You don't need the drink after all?"

"I just didn't want to assume," Natalie said.

"What would you prefer to do?"

He asked it with a hint of humor. It seemed like he had at least some idea of what had crossed her mind – that she might prefer to spend the night making full use of the bed in the airport hotel, that she'd like to feel those arm muscles for herself.

But that was getting way ahead of herself, and hopefully, he couldn't actually read her mind.

"I'd prefer not to drink alone," Natalie said, hoping the way she said it sounded confident, not pathetic.

"Agreed," Garret said.

She restrained herself from thanking him, instead falling into step beside him, heading for ground transportation and the bar in the airport hotel.

"I guess we should go to our rooms first and clean up as best we can before we inflict ourselves on the bar and its patrons," Natalie said.

"If you want." His gaze flicked sideways and over her. Apparently, Garret was having hallucinations, because he seemed to like what he saw. "You don't need to," he said.

"Well I wasn't suggesting it for you. You look like you just stepped out of a Gucci commercial."

Garret's lips twitched. "Weird, but I'll take that as a compliment."

"It'll be nice to put down my backpack so I don't have to

wear it at the bar like I'm part of a really inappropriate 'take your daughter to work day.'"

Garret let out a sudden laugh. She'd forgotten it until just now, but it was part of what she'd always liked about him. It was so full-throated and hearty – his amusement sounded wholesome. He was so clearly laughing with you, not at you.

Natalie smiled, pleased with herself for eliciting the reaction.

"When we're on ground transportation, will you give me your cell number? You're my only friend in Detroit. I don't want to lose you."

Clever reasoning, she thought to herself, thrilled by the idea of exchanging numbers. She nodded agreement.

She was already arguing with herself over whether it was appropriate to be having fantasies of spending the night with him. She'd never had the opportunity in college, had never even had the chance to talk to him alone.

Garret touched her elbow, and when Natalie didn't protest, steered her in the direction of the ground transportation sign. "I can't believe we ran into each other like this," he said. "It almost makes the layover worth it."

"Yeah?" Natalie asked, heart beginning to pound again.

He smiled, the expression as charming as she remembered, with a slight touch of the little boy aiming to please. "You didn't know I had a crush on you?"

Natalie rolled her eyes. "Please. Mr. Captain of the Crew Team, you could have had anyone."

"I thought you only went for the smart ones," Garret said, messing with his phone to call them a Lyft. "Didn't that boyfriend you had – Thomas Linney – he won like a Rhodes Scholarship or something, didn't he?"

"You remember who I dated?"

Garret shrugged.

The inside of Natalie's chest warmed. She would tell him she'd had a crush on him, too, at some point tonight. For now, however, she'd enjoy the sweet validation of hearing what he'd thought about her, listening to how he'd wanted her.

She was buzzing and she hadn't even had a chance to use the drink ticket yet.

Their Lyft pulled up, a silver luxury sedan. Garret opened the door for her, and she felt giddy as she got in. They might be headed to a dingy airport hotel, but the moment made her feel glamorous – staying overnight on the airline after a jetsetting business trip, accompanied by a handsome man who said he'd had a crush on her in college.

"You're right," Natalie said after he'd had a chance to get in on the other side and settle in. "I think this layover might turn out to be a good thing after all."

The Worst Trip Ever

Everything went wrong.

The car broke down on the drive to the vacation rental, but Drew didn't seem perturbed. He used an insurance program attached to his cell phone to rent them a new one and get them back on the road.

Then the vacation rental's keys were nowhere to be found, and they spent hours of a surprisingly chilly summer evening searching beneath every sandy welcome mat surrounding the cottage while trying unsuccessfully to text the owner. But what Ramona would remember later was laughing until she gasped at how ridiculous this was, grinning at Drew until her cheeks hurt.

When they did finally get inside, the California King they'd been promised was no more than a full bed, and a sagging one at that. Ramona and Drew crawled into it gratefully, shedding their clothes as they went. It sagged a lot more in the morning.

In the morning, they discovered that the refrigerator wasn't working, and that a previous guest had left a knot of lunchmeat in the bottom drawer that had turned putrid.

They closed the refrigerator tightly, texted the owner again, shrugged and went outside to see what they could see.

They found a stand on the way to the beach that sold fresh fruit, and Ramona ate so much pineapple that her stomach ached. Still, it was hard to be sorry with Drew fussing over her, encouraging her to spread out on their largest beach tool while he rubbed gentle circles just below her belly button.

"This is the worst trip ever," Ramona sighed. "Nothing is going according to plan."

Drew grinned back at her, looking more handsome than any man had a right to be. The sun did amazing things for his skin, eyes and hair, bringing out layers of depth and shine in the various brown shades that made up his face. Drew seemed to glow from within, and Ramona felt an answering glow in her chest. "What did you plan?"

She wrinkled her nose, laughing. "Nothing, I guess. I just expected things to be easier."

"Are you having fun, though?"

She swatted his arm, but he caught her hand, fixing her with a serious gaze. She shifted uncomfortably, feeling younger than the moment called for. "I always have fun with you."

"Even when everything else is going wrong," Drew said solemnly. He touched each of her fingertips in turn. Slowly, it dawned on Ramona that a momentous thing was about to happen.

A moment later, there was a ring in the palm of Drew's hand, a diamond glittering so brightly in the sun that Ramona had to squint to look at it. "May I put this on your finger?"

"What is it?"

"It's an engagement ring, Ramona. I want all my worst

trips ever to be with you. That way, they'll never really be bad."

A wild part of her wanted to burst out laughing. It seemed impossible that someone as incredible as Drew wanted to spend the rest of his life with her.

But she could see from his eyes that nothing about this was a joke. "Yes, please," she said, wriggling her finger.

The movement startled him, and he dropped the ring in the sand. It took them an hour of searching and cursing to find it again.

It was the worst trip ever, but once they found the ring and it nestled safely on Ramona's ring finger and they had begun to talk excitedly about where they would live and what they would do together as the years passed, Ramona realized that Drew had been right. Nothing could really be bad as long as they always loved each other like this.

She knew then that the worst trip ever was only the beginning of the best life she could imagine.

Happily Ever After

Many times that year, Clara Lawson thought about canceling the annual trip to the island.

She and Rowan had met on the island 25 years before, and they'd traveled faithfully back every year to relive the memories and make new ones. The last week of June had become a cherished time for them both, and Clara usually looked forward all year long to eating at their favorite spots, walking together by the water and curling up with Rowan on a rented balcony to watch the seagulls catch fish.

They'd taken their kids along once they had them, but since both Salome and Terence had left for college, Rowan and Clara had restored the trip to being romantic rather than family-oriented.

This year, however, with Rowan having been sick for so much of it, with the possibility that she might lose him, the thought of the island had lost its usual charm. How could Clara bear to revisit the beginning when she feared their love story might be coming to an end?

A month before they were supposed to leave, when she

needed to pay the deposit on the beach house, she broached the topic to Rowan.

It was hard for her to bring practical matters up with him these days – his illness had thinned and weakened him. It had even shifted the timbre of his voice, making him sound more timid than the man she knew. Now, whenever Clara interacted with him, she saw their remaining time measured too clearly on his face, as if his ashy, sunken cheekbones had become twin clocks, about to mark an hour that was much too late.

Still, she knew Rowan didn't appreciate being coddled or cut out of their mutual life in any unnecessary ways. With the information about the beach house deposit pulled up on her phone, she went into their bedroom to see if he was awake or asleep.

He was awake, though it seemed like he hadn't been for long. His eyes were bleary, and he held his phone closer to his face than he would have normally. He was sitting up, his back leaned against a pile of pillows, his hair sticking up in a way that made Clara ache. It reminded her of Terence as a boy, and of a younger Rowan – who had possessed a careless, charming streak that had never quite faded.

For a moment, she stood speechless, the toes of her bare feet clenching strands of carpet as if that might make it possible to hold onto their life together. Then he lowered the phone and looked at her, and Clara felt she had to explain her presence.

"I have the beach house all set," she said, her voice sounding uncertain in her ears. "But I wondered... we don't have to go if you don't want to." There was so much more she could have said, but any additional words stuck in her throat. Clara swallowed them along with a sob. What had happened to the days when speaking to him was easy as thought, the days when Rowan seemed like an extension of her own being?

Rowan blinked, the gesture made owlish by the dark circles under his eyes. "Do *you* want to?" he asked.

Clara shrugged, her eyes now swimming with tears. "It won't be the same."

"It never has been, but it's always been wonderful." He smiled gently, reaching his arms out to her.

She could not resist the comfort he offered – so often these days, she forgot that it was possible to turn to him. She spent so much of her time trying to care for him, trying to think of ways to make things easier for him.

She joined him on the bed, and Rowan wrapped his arms around her in a gesture that had been familiar for more than two decades. She rested her cheek against his chest, feeling the fabric of his T-shirt, made warm by Rowan's skin and muscle underneath. His heart thrummed in her ear, an affirmation of life that spread through Clara warmly. The scent of him filled her with a sense of home as surely as it had the first time he'd wrapped his arms around her this way, on one of those early nights on the island.

"I don't want to miss it," Rowan whispered into her hair. "I don't want to miss any time I could have with you."

Clara surreptitiously wiped her eyes against his shirt. "Okay," she said, knowing she'd regret it if she gave up this trip – especially if it was the last one they might have together.

"Okay," he agreed, winding his arms more tightly around her.

Clara steered their old Mazda smoothly over the island roads – winding, slow-moving, quaint. The pattern of arriving at the beach house worked on her mind and body as it always did. She felt worry easing from her muscles and brain as she navigated the ocean-side road. Blue went on forever to her left, putting her entire life into perspective. To her right, Rowan sat in the passenger seat, a gray cast to his face but otherwise alert, commenting on the houses that had been built or renovated since the year before.

She could almost believe that everything was all right, and she reminded herself that everything could be all right for now. Rowan was still with her, and they were still together on the island.

The beach house, smaller than the one they'd rented when they used to bring the kids, was little more than a cottage. Gravel turned to sand under the car's tires as she rolled to the end of the driveway to park beside it.

She and Rowan had performed the steps needed to settle into a place like this so many times that speaking wasn't necessary. Clara understood at a cellular level which tasks he would take on, where he would be standing.

She handled her part of things, setting clothes into their borrowed dresser drawers while Rowan transferred food from their cooler to the cottage's refrigerator.

They finished quickly, the years of practice not letting them down.

Then they were left to stare at each other. Clara thought wistfully of activities they used to love that were likely out of reach now – riding bicycles through the seaside forest to the path at the base of the island's lighthouse, or taking a sailboat out onto the bay so they could shout at each other about jib and topsail as if they were seasoned sailors.

Rowan might be on his feet now, but she wasn't sure he

could hold up through those more vigorous activities.

Clara's mouth worked, unsure of what to suggest. She hesitated to sit on the cheerfully colored sofa or test the bed to see how it shifted under her weight. At that moment, she didn't think she could bear staying in the room with him. It would be too easy to reflect on the things that had changed for the worse rather than appreciating what they did have together.

Rowan surprised her by wrapping an arm around her waist, his grip surprisingly strong. "You good to get changed for dinner? We have reservations in an hour."

"Reservations?" Clara raised an eyebrow. "We're starting out fancy, huh?"

"I set dinner up for tonight at The Prime Catch." His expression was as earnest as it had been 25 years ago.

Looking at his face now – as beloved and well-known as it was – the years seemed to fall away for a moment. Clara could see Rowan as he'd been when she first knew him – a young man who still had a great deal of boy in him, no matter how he'd tried to hide it.

She remembered his tone when he'd first asked her to The Prime Catch. They'd been sitting beside each other on the beach, in the position they'd managed to find them-selves in for several days running. The sun was beginning to think about setting, and Clara was beginning to think about how to avoid spending another evening alone.

Rowan had turned to her, his voice deeper than usual, his words slow and serious. He'd told her he'd made reser-vations.

Clara's mind had gone blank from the implications. For some foolish reason, she fixated on the likely cost and protested the expense of the restaurant. Her budget for that first trip to the island had called for her to mostly eat cold cuts from the refrigerator, but that had seemed no hardship when she could spend her days at the beach in the company of the attractive stranger with deep brown eyes and an easy laugh.

Rowan had taken her hand and leaned into her space. He'd only been that close to her a few times at that point, and Clara had held her breath, her fingers trembling in his hold. In those days, any incidental touch sent excitement through the base of her stomach. She had longed to stroke the stubble along his jaw, had dreamed of laying her hand on his arm to compare the different brown shades of their skin.

"I want to take you to The Prime Catch," Rowan had said, in a sexy growl that seemed entirely new. "I want to pay because I want it to be a date. I want to be more than friends."

His eyes had warmed her body everywhere, and Clara had shivered. Still, around the corners of his mouth and eyes, she'd seen the boy in him, the part of him that felt as nervous as she did. Somehow, this made the moment seem real, like something that could belong to her. She was able to hold his gaze and nod slowly. The rest was history.

Now, a quarter century later, she met her husband's eyes and saw that same mixture of man and boy, confidence and uncertainty, and she loved him as fiercely as she ever had. "The Prime Catch is perfect," Clara said.

The Prime Catch was packed, since it was the height of the season. Clara wondered how long ago Rowan had made the reservation.

The aroma of seafood might have been overwhelming

except that one entire wall of the restaurant was open to the ocean. A seaside breeze freshened the experience of the evening and prevented her garlic butter crab legs from overpowering her.

Rowan smiled at her from across the table, the sight of the laugh lines at the corners of his eyes filling her with affection. Whenever she truly stopped to think about what it meant to love a man for two and a half decades, it was almost more than she could comprehend. She'd seen him at his best and at his worst, and she knew she wouldn't trade a moment of it for anything.

"I proposed to you here," Rowan murmured.

"I remember."

He'd asked her permission first, joking that if he was going to strike out, he didn't want to do it in front of a crowd. Clara remembered a few of her friends asking if knowing what would happen at The Prime Catch had ruined the moment – but the truth was far from that. Anticipating his proposal had intensified everything she'd felt that evening.

She remembered sitting across from him 23 years ago, their ankles entwined. Clara had felt terribly grown up, three years into a vacation tradition with a man who would soon become her husband, wearing a dress she'd bought from one of the nicer shops on the island on purpose for the pictures they would soon be taking. It had felt like they were about to embark together on a great adventure – marriage, children, a life by each other's sides.

Even though the Clara of that time seemed little more than a child when she thought back now, everything else she'd been feeling had come to fruition. So often, she and Rowan had not known what they were doing, and yet they'd struggled through it all, right up to this moment.

"I can't imagine what my life would have been if I hadn't loved you," Clara told him.

"Without you, I would have been a different man," Rowan said quietly, his voice almost inaudible under the blanket of other diners. "A lesser man." He leaned forward, pushing a few plates out of the way and intertwined their fingers.

"I know you're scared, Clara," he said. "I am, too. But I wanted to bring you here because this was where I found my happily ever after. All those years ago when I first convinced you to come here. Then when I proposed to you here. Then when we had our 10th anniversary at that table in the corner. So many memories, and a happily ever after every time."

Clara squeezed his fingers so hard her knuckles hurt. "I'm afraid of there being an after."

He lifted his free hand to her cheek. "Clara," he said, putting so much feeling into her name that she couldn't begin to sort out the full meaning of it. "If our time together on this earth has to end, I like to think of you remembering us here together and how we were stronger every time."

She looked away, trying to hold back tears, then felt silly about the effort. She met his eyes, the restaurant and the ocean beyond it falling away. She felt the drops tracking down her cheeks, but she didn't care. She smiled through them.

"You have been the love of my life," Clara said. "It felt like happily ever after the moment I first laid eyes on you."

They laughed together. They could not know how many more days or weeks they would share, but at that moment, the time didn't matter. Clara promised herself that she would enjoy her happily ever after for every moment that it lasted.

Sweet Beginnings Bonus Story

Want more stories of sweet romance? Read on for a bonus story from *Sweet Beginnings: Short Romance Stories About New Love.*

By the Water

Sitting by the water holding a lemonade the size of her head in one hand and an orange cream waffle cone in the other, with her rented one-speed bicycle leaned up against a tree a few feet away, Elsa felt about two decades younger than her thirty years. She wasn't sure if it was the nostalgic flavors taking her back or the way the large items made her hands feel small and undeveloped or the fact that she'd come to this island once with her family as a child, before her parents had gotten divorced. Whatever was causing it, the feeling was a strange mix of excitement and fear – Elsa could see the possibilities that filled the world, but she also felt helpless and overwhelmed in the face of them.

She stared out at the water and tried to find it soothing the way people said it would be. It was much easier to imagine it making her seasick. It moved endlessly, rocking every which way, flashing sunlight into her eyes as it did. Seagulls shouted at each other like couples coming home after having a few too many at the bar. When she looked to her right and left, she saw lots of people sitting on benches doing something similar – desperately trying to relax, sitting uncertainly by rented bicycles with unpredictable brakes, consuming beachside fare in large quantities, acting as if saltwater taffy was an enjoyable thing to have stuck in your teeth.

Maybe this was just the way people felt when they looked up from their phones. Maybe this feeling – the one she was forced to have for the moment because it was going to take like an hour to drink all this lemonade – was what she was avoiding when she picked up her phone to play whatever mobile game she'd downloaded most recently anytime more than 30 seconds passed without a clear action she needed to take. Maybe this feeling would come if she went to bed, closed her eyes and waited to sleep instead of going to bed and looking up high school acquaintances on social media until she passed out with the phone on her chest.

It had been so long since Elsa had tried any of those things that it was hard to remember what she'd been like before having the device. And the only thing keeping her phone out of her hand at the moment was her fear of getting it sticky with lemonade or ice cream or both. People talked about taking screen-free time like it was virtuous – it tended to be discussed in the same conversations as kombucha, meditation, yoga, juice cleanses, microdosing, whatever.

"Do you mind if I sit on this side of the bench?" a man asked.

She glanced up. He had pretty much the same stuff as she did – strawberry lemonade instead of regular, chocolate ice cream instead of orange. But his bicycle looked nicer than hers – it had gears, for one thing. From this, Elsa concluded he was the sort of maniac who owned a bicycle normally. He did have a body to go with that, though – lean muscle that made her eyes a lot less reluctant to dismiss him than her mind was. He had nice hands that looked like he took care of them and thick, chestnut hair that made her want to run her fingers through it.

It was enough to stop her from pretending to have an overwhelming need to stretch out full length on the bench. "Knock yourself out," she said. "I'd slide over, but I'm barely maintaining this ice cream cone as it is."

She licked the orange cream to make the point, but regretted it mid-lick, terribly self-conscious of whether gesturing with her tongue looked sexy or childish.

He graced her with a chuckle. "I'm surprised I was able to walk the bicycle while carrying this thing."

"I was surprised I was able to walk and carry it at all," Elsa said.

They fell silent. She watched out of the corner of her eye as he took in the water. It looked like the sight of the water relaxed him, and she wished intensely that they were close enough for her to ask him about that. How? Why? Was it really the sight of the water that made his face ease and the lines above the bridge of his nose smooth out? Or did he perhaps have a debilitating leg injury and the effects she observed were simply the result of sitting?

"It's so nice to get a little time screen-free, you know?" he said, and Elsa felt a flash of loathing.

"Are you a meditation instructor?"

"What? No. Why do you think that?"

"Screen-free time. It's like people used to preach about removing the toxins from your body and now it's like you should still do that and also remove the toxins from your mind. Like any of us were managing to do the first thing – and now we're supposed to level up and also do the second."

"Did a meditation instructor hurt you?" he asked, the corner of his mouth twitching. "Or do you work for a social media company, and you're angry about anything that might lower your engagement rates?"

She was surprised by the laugh that burst from her at that. She sounded delighted, and the sound made her realize she felt that way, too. The way he'd said it reminded her of something she might say or want to, except that she hadn't expected that reply. Elsa remembered what could be nice about being with another person – how their differences and similarities to your own personality could add depth to an experience, shift your attention, change the way it felt to be sitting staring out at some water.

Indeed, now that she looked at it again, post-laugh, it occurred to her that the glittering of the sun in the ripples was kind of pretty, like what you saw when you really stared into a gemstone. When she was young, she liked to go through her mother's jewelry box and hold the gemstones up to the light one by one, turning them until she found the prettiest angle. Elsa hadn't thought about that in so long that she was amazed she still remembered it.

"Wow, it looks like you're going on a journey," the man said.

"Excuse me?"

"I'll shut up if you want me to," he said immediately. His chastened look, combined with the ice cream and lemonade in his hands, gave her a momentary glimpse into how he might have looked at age seven after being scolded by his mother.

The thought made her feel affectionate toward him. Instead of agreeing that he should shut up, Elsa said, "No, that's okay. What do you mean 'going on a journey?'"

"It just looked like you were having really deep thoughts." He paused and took a long, meaningful sip of his lemonade. "You don't work in social media. You're a theoretical physicist, and you're working out the thing people will be writing popular science books about once we're all tired of string theory."

This time, Elsa's guffaw drew looks from other benches. She wished she could cover her mouth or face, but all she could do was try to figure out how to take a bite of ice cream and make it look demure and well-behaved. Their eyes met over the ludicrously large dome of their ice cream cones, and his sheepish expression told her he'd had a similar impulse. Elsa started to giggle, and it went on an inappropriately long time – except that he did it with her.

When they both contained the laughter, they gifted each other with the smile of true friends and co-conspirators. "I'm actually a code-breaker," Elsa said. "And I think you might be the spy who's come to see if I've found the key."

"No," he said, "I'm a meditation instructor sent by the government to help focus your mind so you can break the code even faster." When he grinned, the skin at the corners of his eyes wrinkled in a way she found appealing.

"Ugh, I hate meditation instructors," Elsa said.

"Oh, no! I really am a meditation instructor." His face fell.

"What?" Guilt blossomed through her chest. She thought they'd been playing. She hadn't meant to insult him. "I'm so sorry."

He set down his lemonade on the bench – why hadn't

she thought to do that? Instead, she'd been clutching it as if she was bound to the enormous cup until all liquid was consumed. With his miraculously free hand, he patted the side of her arm. She liked that the gesture was a little awkward, as if he wasn't quite sure of the angle of approach. That told her that he wasn't the type of man who went around touching strangers all the time. "Don't apologize," he said. "I was messing with you. I was telling the truth earlier when I said I'm not a meditation instructor."

"Earlier?"

"Literally the first question you asked me was whether I'm a meditation instructor."

"Right." Elsa remembered now. "That'll be a weird story to tell our kids," she said, then felt blood rush fiercely to her face as she realized what that sounded like. Her mouth worked soundlessly as her brain tried to catch up and find a way to recover from saying something that made it seem like she'd gone way too far down the road of fantasy about him in her head.

"No, it's a compliment to learn a woman's thinking about bearing my children within moments of meeting me," he said with a broad grin – which quickly turned into a wince. "That made it weirder, didn't it?"

She nodded, feeling the urge to giggle again.

"It sounded so clever in my head," he said.

"Things often do."

He shrugged and leaned back on the bench, making himself at home in a way Elsa wasn't sure she knew how to do, spreading his limbs over it. "I'm not worried, though. If I ever want you to go away, I'll just take up meditation."

"I probably should," Elsa said.

"Take up meditation?"

She wrinkled her nose. "Everyone tells me it would be good for me."

He shrugged. "Or you could try drinking more."

"Or both," she suggested, laughing almost too hard to get the words out. They were grinning at each other like fools, like children. She realized that the discomfort she'd felt sitting by the water had vanished. The evening seemed golden now, the sort of thing she'd remember in another decade or two, an almost surreally perfect moment.

The water ran gracefully onward, gently. It seemed to know exactly where it was going. Its surety comforted her, struck Elsa as an offer of grace.

"Okay," she said, trying to mimic the gestures with which he'd consumed his half of the bench. She set her lemonade down on the ground, feeling more liberated by the act than quite made sense consciously, and focused both hands on holding the ice cream. "I need to know once and for all. Are you or have you ever been a meditation teacher?"

"In the spirit of honesty, I have to inform you that I have a meditation app on my phone."

"Oh my God, I knew it." They'd gotten closer. Elsa had the urge to discard her ice cream and wrap her arms around his neck. She restrained herself, but she was sure something of the idea showed on her face – she thought she could see it on his face, too, like water reflecting the sun.

They stared into each other's eyes - his were blue, faceted like the gemstones she remembered or that water nearby. Their laughter faded and the mood turned serious. "I'm Luke Walton," he said. "I'm here on this trip alone. I don't have a partner or spouse, and I'm wondering if you want to go wait in line with me at the place where everyone says you have to get dinner. I have a feeling the line wouldn't seem nearly as long if we got in it together."

"That was very specific and detailed," Elsa said, though she liked everything about it.

He shrugged without apology.

"I would love to," she said. "Though I have to say I'm not that crazy about this ice cream everyone says you have to buy." She stood decisively, found a nearby trash can, threw the ice cream away, and wanted to shout in triumph. When she returned, he was grinning admiringly, as if she'd accomplished something big.

"You look like a free thinker. Someone who might even order something besides the crab cakes."

"Oh yeah," Elsa said. "I'm going to order a single trip to the salad bar and a large creme brulee cheesecake."

"I don't know if I can handle being that edgy," Luke said.

"I guess you'll have to meditate about it." Elsa picked up her lemonade. She did like that, she decided, taking a large swig of it. And she liked Luke, and she liked who she was with him right at this moment. She wasn't desperately trying to relax anymore – once he showed up, it just happened.

She reached out a hand to help him off the bench and he took it, swinging himself up with an elegance that made her wonder if later she might dare to invite him back to her room. For the moment, she shrugged off the idea. Instead, they both found a rack where they could lock up their bikes. She waited while he finished his ice cream and lemonade.

Then Elsa took Luke's arm with exaggerated comedy and they walked together toward a well-known crab shack where she was now duty-bound to order a trip to the salad bar and a slice of cheesecake. They laughed together like people who trusted each other, and she thought how nice it was to have that, and how incredible it might be to have it longer than tonight.

If you enjoyed this story, look for *Sweet Beginnings: Short Romance Stories About New Love,* available in ebook and paperback editions at your favorite bookseller.

Acknowledgments

My first acknowledgement is always to you. It means more than anything that you have taken the time to read my words.

I'd also like to thank all the people who have made my own getaways pleasant ones. I'm grateful to everyone who works to help people enjoy time away from home, and especially to all people who feel called to host and welcome strangers.

Thank you to Elizabeth Naone for beautiful cover art as always.

Thank you to Paul for being supportive and proud of my writing projects.

Thank you to Lonely Robot Press for continuing to create beautiful editions of my work.

About the Author

Erica Anoe is a hapa haole writer who is interested in exploring characters and places that exist on the borderlands. Born in Kailua, Hawai'i, she currently lives on the mainland and works in cybersecurity.

SWEET ROMANCE

Sweet Beginnings: Short Romance Stories About New Love

If you love the shivery thrill of a crush, you've come to the right place.

The first sparks of attraction, the risk of letting the other person know you're interested, the relief of finding out the other person likes you, too… Beginnings are about possibilities and imagination, and the five romantic stories in this collection are about those sweet first moments.

Meet a former football star whose humiliating failure in the big game has haunted his life ever since – and see how his sister pushes him out of his slump and helps him take the first steps toward finding life and love.

A cynical woman on vacation can't relax – until she finds herself cracking jokes on a bench by the water with an attractive stranger.

An ambitious career woman gives herself permission to pursue her romantic desires, pushing through the shame she feels about her desire for control.

A woman's best friend pushes her to connect for a second time with a handsome man, despite their first date having ended in disaster.

Two people who constantly run into each other as they pursue common interests decide to find out if these chance encounters are actually the whispers of fate.

Enjoy the comfort and hope of couples taking the first brave, tentative steps toward finding love.

TECHNOLOGICAL THRILLER

Design Flaw

Cybersecurity meets high fashion in a stylish trip through an elite and dangerous world.

Christina Yee's life has gone downhill since past glories of Fashion Week in Paris, where she was once famous for adding electronics to designer dresses. Her plan? Hack an exclusive Manhattan event put on by the iconic Princess Zenobia of Nemea.

All she needs is a "borrowed" $15,000 dress, social engineering skills and a quick bypass of a supposedly secure elevator console. From there, Christina knows it'll be a simple matter to hack the show's electronics, make a few signature improvements and collect adulation from all sides. Her return to prominence is assured.

Except that Christina is not the first person to hack this particular network. Christina is quickly drawn into a beautiful and deadly web of far-reaching intrigue. She must push her hacking skills to the limit in order to survive and protect the people she cares about – and she may make a new name for herself in the process.

<u>Queen of the Crossroads</u>

Piper is a Road's Beloved, an eternal traveler who has been given power and destiny by the Road itself. The tangle of birthmarks that cover her skin represent the gifts of every road she has ever walked or will ever walk. They are the source of her magic, and they define her place in the world.

When Piper arrives at Worldsbridge to claim a message from its ruler, she expects a simple encounter. Instead, she finds herself threatened by a bitter king who holds secret grudges against her kind.

To survive, Piper must uncover the true nature of Worldsbridge and learn what the Road expects of those it loves.

"Queen of the Crossroads" is a Road's Beloved short story set in the legendary city of Worldsbridge.

Bridge of Fate

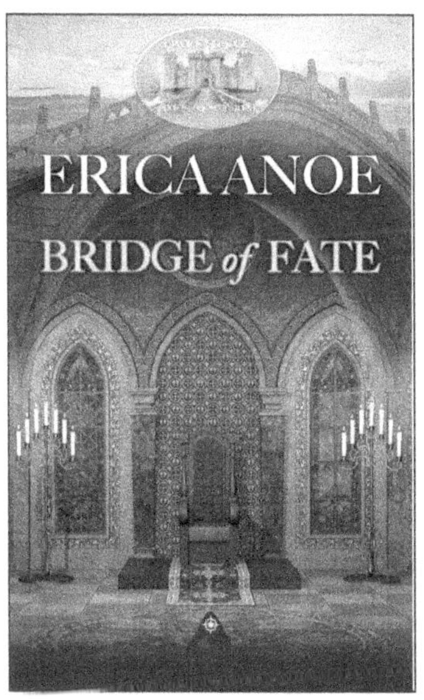

Every night, she dreams of locked doors.

Worldsbridge, the great city where all roads meet, slept for a generation under the rule of a stagnant, mad king. Etta replaced him on Worldsbridge's throne at the command of the spirit of the Road itself, but her fate demands she accomplish even more.

Piper, an immortal traveler who serves the Road, lives a life of leaving. In Worldsbridge, beside Etta, she's finding something that resembles home. The Road, however, is not made for rest.

Together, Piper and Etta must fulfill their destiny and unlock the secret power of Worldsbridge, no matter the personal consequences.

"Bridge of Fate" is a Road's Beloved short story set in the legendary city

of Worldsbridge.

<u>The View From Worldsbridge</u>

In the distance, a traveler approaches Worldsbridge, bringing secrets and change.

Etta, Queen of the Crossroads and ruler of the great city of Worldsbridge, wears her rank uncomfortably. Born in humble circumstances, consumed with loss, she fears she is not capable of becoming the queen the city needs and deserves.

Worldsbridge, the great city where all roads meet, is truly many cities in many worlds, and Etta is responsible for all of them. Neglected for a generation under the rule of a stagnant, mad king, the people of Worldsbridge will no longer stand for the rule of a useless leader.

Etta's fate is bound to the fate of Worldsbridge, and now she must prove before it is too late that she is the true Queen of a mysterious, magical city whose rules she has yet to understand.

"The View From Worldsbridge" is a Road's Beloved short story set in the legendary city of Worldsbridge.

HISTORICAL FICTION

Trapped in the Hold of the SS Madras: A Kingdom of Hawai'i Short Story

"We were not sick with smallpox, but we knew we would be soon if we couldn't get out of this hold."

April 1883. The SS Madras arrives at the port of Honolulu with hundreds of workers for the rice paddies of Waikiki – but it also carries smallpox. Historical fiction set in the waters of the

Kingdom of Hawai'i, "Trapped in the Hold of the SS Madras" tells the story of a steamer mired in uncertainty, a kingdom determined to avoid another plague, and passengers desperate to disembark before they contract a deadly disease.

Includes a historical note by the author with information about the case heard by the Supreme Court of the Kingdom of Hawai'i that inspired this story.